Aisha and Silver

JULIE
SYKES

illustrated by
LUCY
TRUMAN

nosy
crow

To all the friends of Unicorn Academy
and to unicorn lovers everywhere.

First published in the UK in 2021 by Nosy Crow Ltd
The Crow's Nest, 14 Baden Place
Crosby Row, London, SE1 1YW

www.nosycrow.com

ISBN: 978 1 78800 929 4

Nosy Crow and associated logos are trademarks
and/or registered trademarks of Nosy Crow Ltd.

Text copyright © Julie Sykes and Linda Chapman, 2021
Illustrations copyright © Lucy Truman, 2021
Cover typography © Joel Holland, 2021

The right of Julie Sykes, Linda Chapman and Lucy Truman to be
identified as the authors and illustrator respectively of this work
has been asserted by them in accordance with the Copyright,
Designs and Patents Act 1988.

All rights reserved

This book is sold subject to the condition that it shall not,
by way of trade or otherwise, be lent, hired out or otherwise
circulated in any form of binding or cover other than that in which it
is published. No part of this publication may be reproduced, stored
in a retrieval system, or transmitted in any form or by any means
(electronic, mechanical, photocopying, recording or otherwise)
without the prior written permission of Nosy Crow Ltd.

A CIP catalogue record for this book is available from the British Library.

Printed and bound in Great Britain by Clays Ltd, Elcograf S.p.A.

Papers used by Nosy Crow are made from
wood grown in sustainable forests.

1 3 5 7 9 10 8 6 4 2

The rumbling became a roar. Aisha stared in disbelief as the top of the mountain seemed to slide closer. Blinking, she realised a gigantic wall of snow was falling from the top, straight towards them. "Avalanche!" she shrieked.

532 579 85 1

...Where magic happens

HAVE YOU READ?

LOOK OUT FOR:

CHAPTER ONE

The hailstones battered down on the roof, but Aisha ignored them. She and her unicorn, Silver, were safe and warm inside the stables at Unicorn Academy. Aisha's fingers moved quickly along her flute, playing the lively piece of music she had been composing for her dorm's end-of-term display ride. Silver tapped along with his hooves.

Aisha had almost reached the end of the piece when Lily came into Silver's stall. Aisha paused, suddenly realising that the hailstorm had stopped and it was quiet again.

"There you are! I ran over as soon as the

1

storm ended to check you were OK," said Lily.
"The hailstones were massive. There's loads of
damage." Lily tucked her short, dark hair behind
her ears. "Trees have lost branches, the greenhouse
has been smashed." She shivered. "That's the
second hailstorm in two days. It's really worrying.
Zara wants us to have an Amethyst dorm meeting
with our unicorns to talk about what Ms Nettles
said. Are you coming?"

Aisha remembered Ms Nettles, the headteacher,
giving a long speech in assembly that morning,
but she'd been thinking about her music and she'd
drifted off into her own thoughts. Afterwards,
she'd hurried to the stable block to play her
piece to Silver. She frowned. "I'm working on
my music."

"Please, Aisha. This is important. And –" Lily
smiled hopefully – "we're going to play crossnet
afterwards. It's much more fun with four of us."

"Let's go, Aisha," pleaded Silver. "I love crossnet!"

Aisha shook her head. Her friends were great, but when she composed music she couldn't relax until she was happy with it. It was like having an itch she had to scratch. "Sorry," she apologised. "You can tell me what you talked about later." She lifted her flute to her lips.

"OK," said Lily, walking away. "But Zara won't be happy about this."

Aisha continued playing her music while Silver munched on his hay, until the stable door swung open again. Aisha blinked in surprise as she saw Zara, Phoebe and Lily all standing there. Zara's hands were on her hips and her dark eyes were cross. "Aisha," she said sternly, "Lily said you're too busy to come to our dorm meeting."

Behind Zara, Lily gave Aisha an apologetic look.

"I'm working on my music," said Aisha. She put her flute down and tightened her high ponytail.

"Aren't you worried about what Ms Nettles said?" Zara asked.

"It's awful!" exclaimed Phoebe. "Please come with us to talk about it, pleeeeeease!"

Aisha felt her lips twitch. Phoebe was always so dramatic.

"We're not leaving without you," Zara told her.

Aisha grinned. She knew when she was beaten. "All right," she said, putting her flute in its case. "I'll come."

"Yay!" Silver whinnied in delight. "We can play crossnet!" He eagerly trotted over to the other unicorns.

"So, what did you think about what Ms Nettles said?" Zara asked Aisha as they followed Silver. "It's really worrying, isn't it?"

"Um…"

Zara frowned. "Honestly, Aisha! You didn't listen! If the hailstorms get worse then school may have to close."

"Ms Nettles said one of us might be *killed* if we

got caught outside in a hailstorm!" Phoebe's blue eyes widened.

"She didn't exactly say that, Phoebs," said Zara carefully. "She said that if these storms carry on, it will be too dangerous for us to stay at school. The term will have to end early and graduation will be brought forward – we'd all be going home in just five days' time."

"That's terrible!" Aisha hated the idea of saying goodbye to her friends early. Also, she and Silver weren't ready to graduate because he hadn't discovered his magic and they still hadn't bonded. When unicorns and their partners bonded, a strand of the person's hair turned the same colour as their unicorn's mane. Then everyone could see that they were partners – and best friends – for life. If term ended in five days, she and Silver might not graduate and they would have to return to the school for a second year. Much as she loved

Unicorn Academy, Aisha didn't want to stay there without the rest of her dorm.

"We need to find out who's causing these hailstorms and stop them!" declared Phoebe.

Aisha's eyes widened. "You mean the hailstorms might not be natural, they might be caused by magic?"

"Shh!" Zara said hastily, glancing round. "Let's go to the meadow where we can continue our meeting without being overheard!"

CHAPTER TWO

Zara vaulted on to her unicorn, Moonbeam. The others followed her lead and soon they were all cantering out of the stable yard and past Sparkle Lake. The fountain in the middle of the lake brought magical water up from the centre of the earth that then flowed all around Unicorn Island. The water made the crops and animals on the island flourish, and when the unicorns drank it, it strengthened their powers. When students of the academy graduated, they became guardians of the island and helped protect its magical waters. Aisha planned to be a composer or a musician,

but she loved knowing that she and Silver would also work together, protecting their beautiful island.

Near the meadows, the girls passed their riding teacher, Ms Tulip. She was heading for the stables with Mr Longnose, a school inspector. He was a tall, gangly man with a pointed nose and sharp eyes and he always seemed to think he knew best. She felt sorry for Ms Tulip, having to listen to him ramble on as they walked. Poor Ms Tulip!

"Let's not go near Mr Nosey Parker," muttered Phoebe. "He'll only ask where we're going!"

"I don't trust him one bit," said Zara darkly.

Giving Mr Longnose and Ms Tulip a wide berth, they cantered into the meadow. They dismounted next to a sparkling stream and the girls sat down on some nearby tree stumps while the unicorns splashed into the icy water, whinnying and kicking it at each other. Silver

loved to play, and he stamped his hooves harder than anyone, laughing when he soaked the others. Aisha grinned. She loved Silver so much. He was so confident and cheerful.

"Right, Amethyst dorm, down to business!" said Zara, pulling a pen and notebook out of her pocket. "I think someone is making these hailstorms happen and I suspect it's the same mystery person who's caused all the other problems this year – the tornadoes, the tidal wave and the drought. If we want Unicorn Academy to stay open, we need to work out who is responsible and stop them." She opened her notebook. "Let's examine what we know."

"The person doing these things is a man," Lily put in. "We've heard him speak every time there's been a weather disaster."

"*You cannot stop me,*" said Phoebe, making her voice sound deep and spooky, just like the voice they had heard in the aftermath of the weather disasters.

Aisha grinned. "That's a perfect impression, Phoebs!"

Phoebe looked pleased. She loved to act.

"Moonbeam has also seen visions of a man," said Zara. Moonbeam, her unicorn, had magic that gave her glimpses of the future and helped her foresee danger. "He's tall and skinny and wears a cloak. Because of the types of disasters, we can also conclude that our suspect is someone who knows a lot about the weather."

"Mr Longnose!" said Lily. "He's tall and thin and he studied weather and geology before he became an inspector. He's also been sneaking round the school using secret tunnels!"

"And he was with us when the tidal wave hit the coast," said Phoebe. "Remember how he insisted we went camping at that exact spot! He dragged us into danger!"

"Also, we found a book in his tent with notes about how to cause purple tornadoes, volcanic eruptions and droughts," said Zara triumphantly. "That's real evidence!"

Aisha frowned. "But when we showed the notebook to Ms Nettles, she told us that it wasn't Mr Longnose's handwriting and that the initials inside it were 'LT'. Mr Longnose's name is Ivor. His initials are IL. He can't have written the notes in that book, but it is odd he had it in his tent."

"The man's voice didn't sound anything like Mr Longnose's either," said Phoebe. "It was much deeper."

Zara tapped her pen against her mouth. "OK, how about this theory? What if Mr Longnose is working with the LT who wrote the notes in that book?"

"LT!" shrieked Phoebe, leaping to her feet. "Ms Tulip's

name is Larissa so her initials are LT! She and Mr Longnose are always hanging round together at the moment. Maybe they're in league!"

"Phoebe, no! Ms Tulip is lovely. She wouldn't want to hurt the island or the unicorns," protested Lily.

"The voice in the storm definitely wasn't Ms Tulip's voice," Aisha added.

Phoebe huffed. "Oh, this is all so confusing. It's making my head ache."

Zara frowned. "The main thing is that we suspect Mr Longnose is involved somehow. He may very well be working in league with someone. I propose we do some serious spying on him. Agreed?"

"Agreed!" everyone cried.

Zara shut her notebook with a snap. "Good. I declare this meeting closed. Now, crossnet time!"

They jumped up. The crossnet pitch was next to the meadow. While the other girls gathered the unicorns, Phoebe ran to the little hut beside the

pitch and took out crossnet sticks – wooden poles with nets at the top – and the crossnet ball.

Soon the four friends and their unicorns were racing up and down the pitch. Zara and Phoebe were on one team and Lily and Aisha on the other. There were two hoops on the edges of the pitch, suspended from trees. The ball had to be thrown from person to person using the sticks and when a team threw it into their hoop, they scored a point. Magic wasn't allowed, but everyone knew it was more fun if that rule was broken.

"Yay!" Phoebe caught the ball but, just as she aimed for the goal, the ball rose out of her net and floated away. "Oi!" she yelled indignantly.

Lily, giggling, held out her net as Feather brought the ball to them using her moving magic. Seconds before it reached Lily, Zara and Moonbeam galloped in front of them. Zara swung her stick and snatched the ball from the air.

"Faster!" Zara urged, as Moonbeam raced towards the goal. She hurled the ball forward and it dropped through the hoop. "Yay! Goal to me and Phoebs!"

"How did you do that?" spluttered Lily.

Zara grinned. "Moonbeam used her magic to see what you were going to do so we stopped you!"

Lily scooped the ball up with her net and rode to the centre to start the next point. She threw it to Aisha, who caught it. Silver charged towards their goal, but as Aisha threw it at the hoop, the ball seemed to hit something invisible.

Rebounding, it flew straight down the pitch and into Phoebe's waiting net. Phoebe chucked it straight into her and Zara's hoop. "Two-zero!" she whooped. Getting a strong whiff of burnt sugar, Aisha knew Shimmer had used his magic – he could make balls of energy.

"It's not fair!" sighed Silver. "I wish I had magic too."

"We'll find out what your magic is soon," she said.

Silver's ears pricked. "You're right," he said. "I bet I'll discover my powers any day now!"

They started to play another point but as Lily scored, Aisha noticed something. "It's getting really dark."

They all looked up. The sun had disappeared behind heavy black clouds.

Zara looked alarmed. "Those look like hail clouds. We'd better get inside!"

They put the equipment away and set off across the meadow at a gallop. They were only just in time. As they dived into the stables, huge hailstones started to fall. They watched from the doorway as the hailstones dropped like stones and splintered into icy shards on the ground.

"Thank goodness we're not out in that," said Lily.

"Those are definitely not normal hailstones," said Zara grimly. "If this is Mr Longnose's fault, we've got to stop him!"

A man's voice snapped out behind them. "If what is my fault?" They swung round. Mr Longnose was coming out of the tack room with Ms Tulip.

"Nothing!" Zara said quickly.

Mr Longnose gave them a suspicious look. "Hmm."

"Come on now, girls," said Ms Tulip. "There's no point hanging round at the doorway. Settle your unicorns in their stables and then you can sweep the aisles for me."

The girls sighed and set to work.

As Zara led Moonbeam into the stable next to Silver's, she whispered to Aisha, "I bet he *is*

responsible, you know."

Moonbeam's eyes took on a faraway look. She swayed and spoke dreamily. *"Danger comes from the frozen heights… He watches… Revenge is in his heart."*

She blinked. "Oh, I just had one of my visions."

Zara and Aisha exchanged looks. "You said danger was coming and a man who wanted revenge was watching," said Aisha.

Moonbeam shivered. "Yes, I saw a man watching us through a telescope. A tall, thin man."

"Mr Longnose?" asked Zara eagerly.

"I'm… I'm not sure," Moonbeam faltered. "I couldn't see his face. It might have been him."

Zara lifted her chin. "Well, if he's watching us, we're going to watch him back!" she declared. "We're going to solve this mystery once and for all!"

CHAPTER THREE

Dinner that night was steaming bowls of stew with crusty bread followed by delicious sticky toffee pudding. Aisha was scraping up the last spoonful of toffee sauce when Ms Nettles stood up and clapped her hands for silence.

"I'm afraid I have some very bad news. The two hailstorms today smashed most of the equipment in the playpark along with several windows in the school building. The teachers and I have decided that for everyone's safety, Unicorn Academy must close early." Ms Nettles paused as a huge groan went up from the room. "The graduation

ceremony will be brought forward. It will now be in five days' time."

"Five days!" whispered Aisha in dismay.

"That's not much time to find Silver's magic," said Lily anxiously.

Aisha bit her lip.

"Your parents will be informed," Ms Nettles continued. "Please also check the weather carefully every time you go outside. Luckily, no one was hurt today, but it could have been a very different story. If the sky looks threatening, stay indoors. If you do get caught in a hailstorm then find somewhere safe to shelter. Do not try to make it back to the academy until the storm has passed."

As she walked from the hall with the other teachers, the students erupted in noisy chatter.

"What am I going to do?" said Aisha. "Five days isn't long enough to find Silver's magic and

bond with him, and I have to complete the music for our display ride."

"The music is great. Forget about it and concentrate on you and Silver," said Lily.

Aisha felt torn. She wanted to find Silver's magic and bond with him, but she wanted her music for the display ride to be perfect. Then, if she and Silver didn't get to graduate, at least the others would have wonderful music when they performed for the parents.

"Five days isn't enough time to do anything!" exclaimed Phoebe.

"We need to solve the mystery of the hailstorms," said Zara. "If we do that, we'll still have a whole month here. Let's follow Mr Longnose!"

They quickly cleared their plates and left the hall. Mr Longnose and Ms Tulip were talking quietly further down the corridor. Zara nodded to the statue of a unicorn and the four of them

ducked behind it. When Mr Longnose and Ms Tulip headed for the staff cloakroom, the girls followed, hiding in an empty classroom as Mr Longnose and Ms Tulip paused to put on coats and wellies.

"Why are they always together?" whispered Lily.

"I still think she might be in league with him!" Phoebe hissed back.

Zara made frantic shh-ing gestures as Mr Longnose glanced in their direction. He stared around for a moment then said something to Ms Tulip and the two of them went out into the frosty night.

The girls tiptoed after them across the grass. The pair seemed to be heading for the stables. They were talking, but their heads were close together and their voices were so quiet the girls couldn't catch what they were saying. Aisha felt

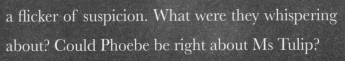

a flicker of suspicion. What were they whispering about? Could Phoebe be right about Ms Tulip?

Suddenly, Phoebe stepped on a frozen puddle and her feet slipped from under her. She shrieked as she fell. Mr Longnose and Ms Tulip swung round.

"Whatever are you all doing?" demanded Mr Longnose, striding over.

"I expect the girls are here to settle their unicorns, Ivor, like they do every night," said Ms Tulip.

"Yes, that's right!" said Zara quickly. "We're here for our unicorns."

"Hmm." Mr Longnose gave them a suspicious look.

"Are you OK, Phoebe?" Ms Tulip asked, as Lily and Aisha helped her up.

"I'm fine, miss," said Phoebe.

"Good. Let's hurry inside, out of the cold," said Ms Tulip.

"Mr Longnose, why are you here?" Zara asked boldly as they all entered the stables. "You don't have a unicorn."

The top of Mr Longnose's cheeks flushed red. "I'm... Um..."

"Mr Longnose kindly offered to help me with evening stables," Ms Tulip said. "Now, come along, girls. It's getting late." She hurried away to the feed room with Mr Longnose following her.

"Suspicious behaviour," Zara hissed to the others. "Very suspicious."

Some more pupils arrived and, under the watchful eye of Ms Tulip, everyone set about making sure their unicorns had fluffy straw beds, full hay nets and clean water.

Silver nuzzled Aisha as she tied up his hay net. "Maybe tomorrow we could go off together and see if we can find my magic," he said hopefully. "I think I'm very close to discovering it. I stamped my hoof earlier and I'm sure I saw a faint pink spark. That's one of the first signs – Feather told me."

"Mmm," said Aisha, not really listening. She was watching Zara and Moonbeam in the next

stable. Moonbeam's eyes were half shut, and she was swaying from side to side.

Silver stamped a hoof. "Aisha, I'm beginning to think you don't care if I find my—"

"Shh," Aisha interrupted, nodding at Moonbeam.

Moonbeam's eyelids were fluttering. "*The tall figure watches with his telescope. Look to the north. Silver... NO!*"

Moonbeam's eyes snapped open in alarm. Aisha and Silver hurried to the partition.

"Was that another vision, Moonbeam?" asked Silver.

Moonbeam nodded. "I saw the cloaked man with a telescope again. I saw you too, Silver, but then you just vanished." She looked worried. "I had a real feeling of danger!"

Silver gulped. "Oh."

"How did he vanish?" asked Zara curiously.

"He just disappeared!" said Moonbeam.

"But where did I go?" Silver said, his voice trembling slightly. For once his confidence seemed to have left him.

"I don't know," said Moonbeam. "Sorry."

Ms Tulip came down the passage between the stables, whistling. The tune made an idea jump into Aisha's head for her piece of music for the display ride. It was jaunty and fun, just what she needed. She hummed a variation of it to herself. Yes – it was perfect!

"Are you done, girls?" Ms Tulip said. "If so, you should be getting back to your dorm."

Aisha's fingers were itching to try the tune out on her flute. "I'm finished, Ms Tulip." She dropped a quick kiss on Silver's cheek. "Night, Silver."

"Wait, Aisha!" Silver pawed the ground. "We need to talk about Moonbeam's vision.

What if I do just disappear?"

Aisha frowned. It wasn't like Silver to worry about things. She hesitated. She really wanted to go and work on her music. He'd cheer up soon, she was sure of it. "We can talk about it tomorrow. Don't worry about it now."

"But—" Silver began.

Aisha didn't stop. "Night, Silver!" she called.

She hurried out of the stable, her mind filled with the melody she wanted to add to her composition. She ran straight back to the dorm, humming to herself as she went.

CHAPTER FOUR

The following morning, the first lesson was geography with Ms Rivers. "Today we are going to learn about tornadoes," she told the class. "Mr Longnose is an expert on weather conditions and has offered to show us an experiment. He's waiting for us outside."

They followed Ms Rivers out to the stable yard. Zara nudged Aisha. "An expert on weather conditions," she muttered darkly. "Do you think that includes using weather to wreck the island? I wonder what he knows about hailstorms!"

Aisha had to admit that it seemed suspicious.

As the class gathered around him, Mr Longnose clapped his hands together pompously. "Today we shall look at tornadoes and the effects of combining magic and science. As I hope you know by now, some magic reactions and some scientific ones are reversible, but not when the magic and science are combined."

Aisha started to think about her piece of music as Mr Longnose droned on. She was pleased with the additions she'd made the night before and couldn't wait to play it to Silver. Zara nudged her and she realised everyone was following Mr Longnose to a nearby water trough.

"Firstly, I'm going to demonstrate how we can create a mini tornado in this bottle using science." He picked up a large glass jar with a screw-top lid from beside the trough. It was filled with water.

"Watch carefully, please." Mr Longnose unscrewed the lid and added a few drops of green liquid.

"What's that, sir? Is it a magic potion?" asked Spike from Topaz dorm.

"No," said Mr Longnose in his usual clipped tones. "It's a simple detergent and the sparkly powder I'm adding now is purple glitter to help you see the tornado." He screwed the lid on to the jar tightly and, turning it upside down, he spun it in a circular motion then held it still. "Observe, a mini tornado in a jar." He brought it closer so they could all see. "Look, Aisha," said Zara, nudging her.

Aisha stared at the tiny glittering tornado

34

whirling in the water, momentarily distracted from her music. "That's so cool!"

Mr Longnose looked pleased at the response. "Spinning the jar as I did created a water vortex that looks like a mini tornado. Science is a wonderful thing, and when scientific knowledge is combined with magic, the possibilities are endless!" His eyes lost their usual sharp, disapproving expression and his face lit up.

"What do you mean, sir?" asked Johan, Spike's friend.

"We can use science to amplify magic, or magic to amplify science, making the effects bigger and stronger!" Mr Longnose said enthusiastically. "When I was a researcher, I worked alongside the brilliant Count Lysander Thornberry."

"Not him again," muttered Phoebe. Mr Longnose was always going on about the count, a scientist and inventor who lived as a recluse.

"The rain machine he made was a major breakthrough in using science to amplify magic," Mr Longnose went on. "The count took rain seeds – magic seeds from the ocean that can make it rain – and created a machine that not only amplified the effect of the seeds so that more rain fell, but that also allowed the count to direct the rainfall wherever he wanted. It was astonishing." He sighed. "The count could have achieved so much if he hadn't decided to closet himself away in his castle, refusing to share his work any further." He shook his head disapprovingly. "A brilliant but flawed man."

Zara put up her hand. "Sir, are you going to combine magic and science today?"

"I am," Mr Longnose said. "Phoebe, please will you fetch Shimmer from his stable?"

Looking surprised, Phoebe went to get her unicorn. Mr Longnose beckoned to him. "I need

your help, Shimmer. Will you please use your magic when I ask?" Shimmer nodded and blew his long pink and blue forelock out of his eyes.

"Everyone, observe the mini tornado." Mr Longnose spun the jar again then held it up for everyone to see. The water tornado twirled gently. "Now, Shimmer, please use your energy magic to make the tornado spin faster. Just a small amount will do."

Shimmer stamped his hoof. A small ball of energy shot into the air and hit the jar. The bottled tornado immediately grew bigger and spun faster. "See!" cried Mr Longnose, as the jar vibrated in his hands. "Keep back!" he ordered. He put the jar down and backed away.

"Again, please, Shimmer!" he called as the jar rattled.

Shimmer stamped his hoof. A larger ball of energy hit the jar.

A sharp crack rent the air and the jar's lid flew across the yard. Everyone gasped as a glittering funnel of whirling water shot upwards, drawing in water from the nearby trough and growing to two metres, before suddenly bursting into a cloud of sparkling raindrops that soaked them all.

"Behold the power of magic and science!" Mr Longnose bowed and held out his hand, motioning for Shimmer to bow too. The class whooped and cheered. Mr Longnose beamed, looking nothing like his usual stuffy self.

"Putting science and magic together is amazing, sir!" said Spike.

"I want to have a go!" said Phoebe.

Mr Longnose's eyes gleamed. "There is practically no limit to the amazing things that can be done when a unicorn who has Shimmer's extraordinary power combines his magic with science."

Even strict Ms Rivers looked impressed. "That was a fascinating demonstration, thank you very much, Mr Longnose," she said warmly. "Now, inside, everyone and I'll give you some homework!"

When Ms Rivers dismissed them for break, Aisha didn't go with the others to get something to eat. Instead she hurried straight back to the stables to see Silver.

"I made some changes to my music last night. Can I play it to you?" Aisha was already pulling her flute from its case. She blew softly into it, closing her eyes as the music took her over. When she'd finished, she smiled to herself. "What do you think?"

Silver rubbed his head on her arm. "It's brilliant."

"Really?" Aisha's chest swelled with pride. "You're not just saying that? Which bit did you like best?"

"All of it. It's perfect," said Silver.

"But...?" prompted Aisha, sensing there was more.

Silver let out a long breath. "I can't stop thinking about what Moonbeam said about me vanishing. It

scared me. You said we could talk about it today, but you haven't mentioned it."

Aisha tried to hide her disappointment – she'd thought Silver was going to say something more about her music. "I really wouldn't worry about it. Moonbeam's visions are hard to interpret. I'm sure you're not actually going to disappear."

"But what if I do?" said Silver doubtfully. "What if I'm kidnapped or something?"

"Aisha!" The rest of Amethyst dorm called her.

Aisha went to the stable door. "I'm here. What's up?" she said, seeing their excited faces as they came piling down the aisle to the Amethyst dorm stables.

"Ms Nettles just made an announcement," said Zara. "Because of graduation being early, lessons have been cancelled so people can practise their displays. Then tomorrow there's a picnic ride to the ruined tower."

"Or students can spend time with their unicorns, trying to bond and find their magic," put in Lily.

"I know," said Phoebe suddenly. "Ms Rosemary said she's got some new mane crayons that we can use to decorate our unicorns for the display. They're like hair dye only better because they wash out. Let's ask if we can practise with them. It'll be fun and it'll give you and Silver some time together to try and find his magic."

"Oooh, yes," said Silver, tossing his mane. "I'd like that."

"Sounds good to me!" said Zara.

"OK," sighed Aisha. She could tell from Silver's hopeful look that he liked the idea of having a pamper session and going on the picnic ride the following day.

"I'll go and ask Ms Rosemary where the crayons are," said Phoebe.

Five minutes later, she came back with a big

box full of hair crayons and glittery hoof polish in different colours. "You just rub the crayons on the mane or tail, Ms Rosemary said, and then after half an hour they set. They'll wash out with hot water. It sounds simple enough! I'm going to turn Shimmer's mane and tail gold!"

They all got together with their unicorns and spent ages having a full-on pamper session.

Aisha painted pink glitter on Silver's hooves then coloured his mane and tail. "You look just like Shimmer usually does," she giggled as she changed his green, red and silver mane and tail to pale pink and blue.

Silver tossed his mane in delight. "I like it. It's fun to look different!" He nuzzled her. "I can't wait until we bond and you get a green, red and silver streak in your hair to match my real mane and tail colour."

Aisha smiled. "Me too."

After their pamper session, the Amethyst girls and their unicorns went for a ride in the academy grounds. Aisha and Silver had fun even though Silver didn't seem any closer to discovering his magic. In the afternoon, the dorm decided to spy on Mr Longnose in the stable block.

"What's he doing now?" hissed Zara as they

peered out from behind a stack of hay bales.

"Counting buckets," Aisha said.

"I can see that, but why?" said Zara.

"Maybe he likes buckets?" suggested Phoebe.

Lily snorted with laughter. Mr Longnose swung round. They all ducked back behind the bales.

"It's OK, he's not coming over," hissed Zara, peeping out.

Mr Longnose tucked his clipboard under his arm and strode down the aisle.

"He's going into that empty stable," Zara whispered. They tiptoed after him and were almost at the door when Mr Longnose darted back out.

"I knew it!" he cried triumphantly. "I thought I was being spied upon! Zara, Phoebe and Lily – you will come with me to Ms Nettles right now. Unicorns, back to your stables immediately!"

He ushered Zara, Phoebe and Lily towards the

stable entrance but completely ignored Aisha.

Aisha stared at Silver in confusion. "What's going on? Why has he left me behind?" she whispered as Mr Longnose marched the others away.

Silver looked puzzled "I don't know."

"I'd better go with them," said Aisha.

She hugged Silver then ran after the others. She wasn't going to let them take all the blame when she'd been involved too.

"Where did you and Silver go?" Zara whispered, looking impressed. "Next time, I'm hiding with you!"

Aisha was confused. "What do you mean? We weren't hiding."

"Silence!" snapped Mr Longnose. "No talking! The head shall deal with you!"

Ms Nettles was very angry when Mr Longnose

told her what had happened. "Girls," she said, after he had left. "I am very disappointed in you. I thought that I made it quite clear, after the summer drought, that Mr Longnose is not causing these events and he has nothing to do with them either. I also made it clear that you were to leave any further investigating to me.

I will *not* have you hounding Mr Longnose in this way. He has the very best interests of both the academy and Unicorn Island at heart. Please leave the inspector alone or there will be serious repercussions. Do I make myself clear?"

"Yes, Ms Nettles," the girls chorused sheepishly.

"As a punishment, you will have a detention in the library tomorrow with Mr Longnose supervising," said Ms Nettles.

"But everyone else is going on the picnic ride!" protested Zara.

"Well, maybe you should have thought of that before you started making a nuisance of yourselves," said Ms Nettles tartly. "Detention tomorrow, girls, and that's that!"

CHAPTER FIVE

Phoebe groaned as she leafed through a big pile of books in the library the next morning. "I wish we were out riding instead of being cooped up here."

"Me too," sighed Aisha. She wished she could be playing her flute instead of writing reports on extreme weather for Mr Longnose. He would be back in a few hours and would expect the work done by then.

"There's nothing about magic hailstorms in these books," said Lily. "I thought this detention might be a good chance to try and find out more

but all the hailstorms I've read about are normal ones."

"This is interesting," said Zara, holding up a thick leather book. "It's about avalanches."

"So's this," said Aisha. "It's all about the Frozen Wastelands, where there are lots of dangerous things like avalanches and sabre-toothed bears. There's also a glacier that has special pink diamonds trapped under the ice. If you find one, you can use it to undo any freezing spell, no matter how strong. It sounds like an amazing place."

"This one mentions the Frozen Wastelands too," said Lily, holding up a very old, thin book. "It was tucked behind another book at the back of the bookshelf. It's a biography about Count Thornberry. It says he has a secret laboratory in the ice caves of the Diamond Glacier."

"He's the person Mr Longnose is always going on about, isn't he?" said Aisha.

"I thought he lived in the south of the island," said Zara.

"His family castle is there but his lab is in the Frozen Wastelands according to this," said Lily. "It says he's worked in secret since he left the university."

She read straight from the book: "*The count was furious when leading scientists questioned his methods, worried that he could unbalance the natural world by using magic to amplify science. Angered by this criticism, the count became a recluse and refused to share his work with the rest of the scientific community.*" Lily turned the page. "There's a picture of him here. He looks pretty weird – look at that moustache!" She turned the book round to show everyone.

Phoebe squealed. "Oh my gosh!"

"What?" demanded Zara.

"Look at him!" said Phoebe, jabbing her finger at the picture. "He's tall and thin and wearing a cloak. Could he be the man Moonbeam sees in her visions?" She ticked things off on her fingers. "He fits the physical description. He's clever. He's angry with people on the island, which could mean he wants revenge. He knows about weather…"

Zara pointed at the picture. "And look at this design embroidered on the pocket of his cloak." She gasped. "It's just like the one on the button we found in that ruined cottage, near to where the tidal wave hit!"

"Lysander Thornberry," said Lily quickly. "LT. Those were the initials in the notebook about weather disasters that we found in Mr Longnose's tent!"

"You know what this means?" exclaimed Phoebe. "Drum roll, please!" She drummed her hands on the desk. "I absolutely bet that we have just found out who Mr Longnose is in league with!"

Aisha stiffened. A drum roll would be perfect for the climax of her piece of music. She tried to fit one into the music in her head. Yes! It was the final flourish she needed! She was so excited, she barely heard the rest of her friends' conversation.

"It's a good theory, Phoebs," said Zara, "but we need actual evidence before we go to Ms Nettles. She's cross enough with us as it is. I vote when we write our reports, we don't put in any of this stuff about Count Thornberry. We don't want to alert Mr Longnose and make him think we're on to him. Let's keep this between ourselves for now, agreed?"

"Agreed," chorused Lily and Phoebe.

"Aisha?" said Zara. "Do you agree?"

"Yes, of course," said Aisha, busy thinking about drum rolls.

Zara smiled. "Great. Let's get our reports written up and then we can be free from detention!"

They all started to write apart from Aisha, who started humming again and tapping her fingers on the desk.

"Aisha! Write!" Zara ordered, handing her a pen. "Unless you want to stay in here all day!"

Aisha definitely didn't want to do that! Grabbing the nearest book, she started to write her report.

When Mr Longnose returned, he took their work with a disgruntled sniff. Whooping for joy, the girls raced outside to the stables. On the way to Silver's stall, Aisha grabbed a handful of sky berries for him, stuffing them in her pocket as a treat for later.

"Silver! I think I've finally finished the music!

Will you listen to it? We can go in the barn – it'll be quieter there."

They went into the barn next door to the stable block. Aisha shut the door behind them and they settled behind the piled-up bales of hay.

"I can finally play you the whole piece now," said Aisha, feeding him some of the berries.

"All right," said Silver, gobbling them up. "But then I want to talk to you. Moonbeam had another vision while you were doing your detention. She said she saw me vanish again."

"Mmm," said Aisha, only half listening as she got her flute out of its case.

"Please, Aisha. I really do want to talk about this. I'm worried," said Silver. "There was a plot to kidnap unicorns a year ago and –" He broke off as they heard adult voices outside the barn door. "It's Mr Longnose and Ms Tulip!"

"Shh," said Aisha. "They're probably just

getting a bale of hay." She stroked Silver's mane as the door creaked open.

Mr Longnose and Ms Tulip came in and shut the door behind them.

Ms Tulip giggled. "Why are we here, Ivor?"

"I needed to talk to you in private, somewhere there are no prying eyes or listening ears," said Mr Longnose. "This is very important."

Aisha stiffened. What was Mr Longnose about to say? She leaned forward to listen, her heart pounding. But as she did so, she dropped her flute and it clattered to the ground.

Aisha quickly grabbed it. She and Silver exchanged horrified glances.

"What was that?" Mr Longnose snapped.

"I don't know," said Ms Tulip.

"What should we do?" Aisha mouthed to Silver.

Silver looked round desperately but there was nowhere they could hide. A smell of burnt sugar wafted through the air.

"The noise came from over there!" Mr Longnose strode across the barn.

Aisha froze. She and Silver were about to be discovered! She hugged Silver's neck and buried her face in his thick mane as Mr Longnose peered around the hay bales…

CHAPTER SIX

Aisha expected to hear Mr Longnose bellow her name but to her utter astonishment she heard him say, "There's nothing here, Larissa."

She looked up from Silver's mane. Mr Longnose was looking straight at her but he turned back to Ms Tulip without acknowledging her at all. "I don't know what caused that noise but there's no one here. Now, Larissa…" Mr Longnose took several deep breaths. "I am so happy that I came here to inspect Unicorn Academy because it has led to me meeting you." Aisha peeped out from behind the bales and saw him blush. "Yes, you,

Larissa Tulip. You fill me with more joy than you could ever imagine. I love you." He cleared his throat. "Dare I… Might I… Is it possible to believe you feel the same?"

"Oh, Ivor! Yes! Yes, I do!" cried Ms Tulip. She hurried over to him and took his hands. "I love you, Ivor Longnose!"

They beamed soppily at each other and then … they kissed!

Aisha's mouth fell open. Mr Longnose and Ms Tulip were *in love*?

Mr Longnose pushed a strand of hair behind Ms Tulip's ear and offered her his hand. Smiling at him, she took it and they walked out of the barn.

"Oh. My. Goodness!" Aisha breathed slowly. "I really wish I could unsee that."

Silver looked just as shocked as she felt. "Totally!" He shut his eyes and shook his head.

"They're in *lurve!*"

"I can't believe it! And why did Mr Longnose carry on talking to Ms Tulip when he knew we were here behind the bales?" Aisha said. "We need to talk to the others about this!"

They were hurrying across the barn when the door opened and the rest of Amethyst dorm and their unicorns looked in.

"There you are!" cried Zara. "We've been searching for you everywhere. What are you doing in here?"

"That doesn't matter," said Aisha. "Just wait till you hear what we just saw!"

"Mr Longnose loves Ms Tulip!" exclaimed Silver.

"No!" squealed Phoebe.

"Yes!" Aisha quickly explained. There were howls of laughter when she got to the kiss.

"That's totally gross," said Phoebe. "Ms Tulip's lovely. She's far too nice for Mr Long*nosey*."

Lily frowned. "What I don't get is why he didn't tell Aisha and Silver off for spying on him? And why didn't he tell them to get out of the barn?"

"I have absolutely no idea," said Aisha. "He just seemed to look right through us – it was like we were invisible."

Phoebe rounded on Aisha. "That's it! Silver has invisibility magic! There's a boy in my drama club at home whose unicorn has invisibility magic – it's so awesome."

"It would explain why I keep seeing Silver vanish!" said Moonbeam.

"But Silver didn't vanish, I could see him the whole time," argued Aisha. "And even if Silver could turn invisible, surely Mr Longnose would have seen me?"

"Not if you were touching Silver!" exclaimed Phoebe. "If a unicorn has invisibility magic and their partner is touching their mane, then they

also turn invisible."

Silver gave Aisha an excited look. "I felt a tingling in my hooves just before Mr Longnose looked round the bales. I desperately wanted to help you hide. I was so worried you were going to get into trouble. Maybe I have got invisibility magic."

"Invisibility magic would explain why Mr Longnose didn't see either of you when he caught us spying on him the other day," said Lily.

"Try it now," urged Zara.

Silver took a breath and stamped a hoof on the ground. A sugary smell filled the air and pink sparks swirled around his and Aisha's legs. His eyes widened and Aisha gasped.

"Wow!" breathed Zara. "Your legs have vanished!"

Silver stamped again and Aisha saw her friends' eyes widen.

"They've gone!" cried Lily.

"We can't see you at all!" said Zara. "Are you still there?"

Aisha grinned and gently tugged Silver's mane, motioning with her head. He nodded, understanding what she wanted to do. They tiptoed behind Zara. "BOO!" Aisha exclaimed.

Zara shrieked and jumped a metre in the air. Silver stamped his hoof again.

"We can see you now!" cried Phoebe as Silver and Aisha burst out laughing.

Zara joined in. "Invisibility magic is totally insane!" She high-fived Aisha.

"You know what this means?" said Lily in delight. "You just need to bond and then you can graduate."

"Hooray!" Silver whinnied but broke off as the barn door slammed open and an icy wind swirled inside.

"What's happening?" said Phoebe as the wind

formed a funnel and moved towards them. Loose hay and dust from the floor were pulled into it, spinning round faster and faster.

"Twisters don't just suddenly form inside a barn," said Zara uneasily. "Everyone on their unicorns, now!"

The girls vaulted on to their unicorns, but the wind had already reached Silver. It encircled him and Aisha and a familiar voice echoed out. *"I've been watching you. I want you. Come!"*

"Help!" yelled Aisha, as she and Silver were lifted into the air.

"Aisha!" Zara shrieked. She grabbed Aisha's coat just as Phoebe and Lily grabbed on to Silver's mane and the cyclone instantly whirled all of the girls and their unicorns away.

CHAPTER SEVEN

The girls clung to each other tightly as they spun round. Suddenly, they dropped and landed with a bump. The freezing air bit into Aisha's cheeks as she stared at the strange, frozen world around them.

"Where are we?" As she spoke, her breath froze in a cloud of ice crystals. She spotted a glint of something pink near her feet. She picked it up. "A pink diamond! I read about them in detention. They can melt anything. They're only found on the Diamond Glacier in the Frozen Wastelands!"

The glacier was covered by a thin smattering of

snow and underneath, thick ice glistened. They were a little way down from the peak of a huge mountain. A fine mist swirled over the glacier and snow-covered cliffs rose up on either side of them.

"But why are we here? And what was that twister? Where did it come from? Ouch!" cried Lily, as a ball of ice fell from the sky and hit her arm. Another fell and then another. Dark clouds were massing overhead.

"It's a hailstorm!" whinnied Silver.

"Quick, over there!" Zara shouted. She pointed to a dark opening beneath a rocky overhang.

They scrambled across the glacier. Once everyone was safely inside the large cave, the girls dismounted. Aisha shivered. The walls were crusted over with ice and pointed white icicles hung from the ceiling like dangerous, jagged teeth. At the back of the cave, a tunnel led further into the mountain.

"That storm is lethal!" said Phoebe, as the hail pounded down outside.

"It's not the only thing that's lethal," said Zara worriedly. "Sabre-toothed polar bears live in the Frozen Wastelands. They attack on sight." She looked round. "I hope one doesn't live in this cave."

"Why are we here?" Lily said. "Did you all hear that voice in the twister?"

Phoebe nodded and mimicked it. *"I've been watching you. I want you. Come!"*

"Someone obviously used magic to bring us here," said Zara grimly.

There was a laugh from behind them and a flash of green light. "Not just magic, but magic and science combined!" They all swung round as a very tall man in a long black cloak stepped out of the tunnel at the back of the cave. He had a pointed moustache and slicked-back dark

68

hair. Silver rings flashed on his long fingers as he rubbed his hands together. "Welcome to my domain!"

"Count Thornberry!" gasped Aisha, recognising him from the picture in the book.

"Indeed!" the count bowed. "I brought you here using a wind created by one of my weather machines."

Zara was outraged. "You kidnapped us? Why?"

"Because I need one of you," the count said.

"Which one?' demanded Zara.

"The unicorn who is the energy thrower. The one with the pink and blue mane who destroyed my tidal wave." The count pointed at Silver, his eyes gleaming. "I have been watching you from afar using a magic telescope. Your power is extraordinary. If I use it to amplify my inventions, I will be able to bring this island to its knees!"

Aisha realised the count had made a mistake.

He thought Silver was Shimmer because Silver's mane and tail was now coloured pink and blue from the hair crayons. "But that's not—"

Silver cut her off. "What do you want me to do?" he asked boldly, stepping forward.

Aisha stared at him. Why was her unicorn pretending to be Shimmer? Silver's eyes met hers briefly and he winked. She hoped that he had a plan, and felt sick at the thought of him putting himself in danger.

The count addressed Silver. "With your energy magic and my weather machines, we can create the biggest ice storm ever. The purple tornadoes, the tidal wave, the heat wave, they were merely practice for the main event. This winter storm will cover Unicorn Island in a solid sheet of ice. Neither science nor magic could achieve such a feat on their own. When we succeed, I, Count Lysander Thornberry the Eighth, will be taken seriously at last!"

The girls' shocked silence was broken by a ferocious roar. A huge sabre-toothed polar bear was in the entrance to the cave. Its small eyes gleamed and long tusk-like teeth curved out of its mouth. Phoebe and Lily screamed and the unicorns whinnied in alarm.

The bear's tiny eyes blazed with fury and it reared up, slashing at the air with claws as long as swords. It opened its cavernous mouth and roared again.

Quicker than lightning, the count pulled a small instrument from his pocket. Holding it steady, he pressed a blue button. A jet of water arced across the cave and covered the angry bear. As the droplets of water hit the bear's fur, the water froze and the bear slowed and stiffened in place, becoming an ice statue.

The count smiled but the smile did not reach his eyes. "That is just a small example of what I can

do. Come with me, energy unicorn," he ordered, pointing at the tunnel behind him.

"No," said Silver bravely. "You can't make me help you."

The count glanced at the frozen sabre-toothed polar bear, then, holding up the portable weather machine, he aimed it at Silver. "I think I can."

Silver stood his ground. "I won't be able to help you if you freeze me."

Count Thornberry moved the machine so that it pointed at the others. "That's true, but I don't need your friends. I shall imprison them and, if you don't help me, you can watch them turn to ice." A twisted smile spread across his face. "One by one!"

CHAPTER EIGHT

Count Thornberry aimed his weather machine at the group and pressed a grey button.

"No!" Shimmer whinnied in alarm.

Aisha gasped, convinced they were about to be frozen, but instead a tornado spiralled out of the machine and swept towards them, getting bigger by the second.

"Run!" cried Zara. But before they could try and escape, the freezing wind had swept them up. Aisha felt like a marble being catapulted down a twisty tube. Several breathless minutes later the wind started to slow. Aisha felt Silver nudge her

urgently. "Aisha! Hold my mane!" he whispered.

She grabbed hold just as the wind died and they dropped to the ground. Aisha's legs wobbled as she clambered to her feet, still hanging on to Silver's mane. She saw they were at the end of a tunnel outside a cave that had a door made of metal bars. Green glowing icicles hung from the ceiling, providing the only light. The count was facing them. Aisha smelled a whiff of burnt sugar and was suddenly sure that Silver was using his magic.

He started to back slowly away from the others. Aisha moved silently beside him. She wished she knew what he was planning but she trusted him completely. She could feel Silver breathing heavily. Doing magic took a lot of effort when unicorns first discovered their powers. She rubbed Silver's neck, silently sending him her love and support. Silver nuzzled her gratefully.

"Get inside," said the count, waving his device.

"No, wait!" He took a step forward. "There were eight of you. Now there are only six. Where's the energy unicorn and his partner? What have you done with them?"

Aisha held her breath as she saw the others look around and realise the count was right. *Please let them work out what we've just done*, she prayed.

Phoebe suddenly stomped forward, looking outraged. "What have *we* done with them?" she cried. "First you kidnapped us from our school and now you've brought us down to this dump, losing our best friend and her unicorn on the way. It's not what *we've* done with them, it's what *you've* done!"

"Your magic machine must have left them behind!" Zara shouted, joining in.

"Pah!" the count spat. "Get in that cave and I'll go and fetch them!"

They filed inside. The count slammed the metal door shut and turned a key in the lock, then he

marched away, his black cloak rippling behind him. As his footsteps grew fainter, Silver let out a sigh.

"Phew! I wasn't going to be able to keep us invisible for much longer!" He leaned against the icy wall, panting for breath.

"You were brilliant." Aisha kissed his neck. She searched in her pocket and found a few remaining sky berries from earlier. "It's not much, but these might help."

Sky berries gave unicorns strength and helped to replenish their magic. Silver gobbled them up gratefully.

"Aisha! Is that you and Silver out there?" Zara hissed through the door.

"Yes! Silver used his magic to trick the count," said Aisha, hurrying to the bars.

"Ha!" said Phoebe. "The count's not as smart as he thinks!"

"Definitely not. He left the key in the door," said

Aisha. The lock was stiff, and it took both hands to turn the huge key but, finally, there was a click and the door swung open. The others raced out, apart from Moonbeam, who was swaying on the spot.

"Beware the falling ceiling… Watch for the spears of ice… Take the left turn…"

A grating noise rent through the air. Glancing up, Aisha saw a crack run across the ceiling. "Maybe he is quite clever!" she gasped. "I think the cave might have a spell on it and it's just noticed you've gone!"

"Moonbeam!" cried Zara.

Moonbeam jerked out of her vision. She cantered out. Zara leapt on to her back. "Gallop!" she shrieked. "Before the roof comes down!"

The walls began to shake as the crack spread along the ceiling of the tunnel. The unicorns hurtled along the icy passageway, the girls clinging on desperately as the crack snaked after them.

The glowing icicles smashed down one by one as the crack passed them. The unicorns raced by a brightly lit lab in an enormous cavern. It must be where the count ran his experiments! But they couldn't stop. They had to get out! The crack was outpacing them now. Aisha shrieked as one of the icicles fell right at Silver's hooves.

The tunnel began to widen. Aisha glimpsed two tunnels ahead, one leading to the left and one to the right. The one to the right had extra-long icicles hanging from the ceiling and there was a frozen bear in the entrance. "That's the way out!" she shouted. But as she spoke, the crack in the ceiling finally overtook them. Moonbeam pulled up suddenly and the other unicorns almost crashed into her, their hooves skidding across the ice.

"Turn back, NOW! That cave was in my vision!" whinnied Moonbeam. She swung round,

forcing everyone away from the tunnel. "Back! Back!"

Just as they retreated there was a colossal *whump* and the icicles hanging from the ceiling of the tunnel all fell like deadly spears.

Phoebe's face was whiter than the ice. "That was close! Imagine if we'd been in there!"

"I think you just saved our lives, Moonbeam," said Feather shakily.

"We've got to find another way out," said Zara.

"Moonbeam, you said *turn left* when you were having your last vision," Lily said. She pointed to the left-hand tunnel. "Let's go left."

They set off again.

"Faster, Moonbeam!" urged Zara.

They galloped along the twisty tunnel, the unicorns' hooves slipping and sliding.

"Crevasse ahead!" Zara yelled over her shoulder, as they approached a gaping crack in the ground.

Moonbeam leapt into the air and cleared it.

Aisha caught her breath as Silver leapt too. For a terrifying moment, the crevasse stretched beneath them, a black void, but then Silver landed safely on the other side. Fresh air blasted Aisha as they followed Zara around a bend. Daylight streamed in from a wide opening. A few steps later and they were galloping out on to the glacier with its snow-covered cliffs on either side.

Phoebe whooped. "We made it! We escaped!"

Looking higher up the glacier, Aisha saw the frozen sabre-tooth polar bear at the entrance to the cave where they had met Count Thornberry. She flung her arms round Silver and hugged him tight. "Silver, you're amazing! I was terrified when you said you were Shimmer. But you were so brave. Your idea of turning invisible to help everyone escape was genius, and –" A shudder ran through her – "I was so scared, I thought the count was

going to do something horrible to you."

Silver nuzzled her. "I felt just the same when I thought he might turn you into ice. I don't know what I'd do if something happened to you."

Aisha buried her face in his mane. Suddenly she realised that though her music was important, nothing in the world mattered as much as Silver did. "Oh, Silver, I'm so sorry. I didn't listen when you wanted to talk about how worried you were that Moonbeam had seen you vanish. I promise I'll always listen in the future. You're the most important thing in the world to me."

"More important than music?" asked Silver shyly.

"Even more important than that," said Aisha.

Silver snorted happily. "And I'm sorry that I worried you. I can be impulsive at times. In future, I'll try to tell you what I'm planning before I do it."

Anxiously, Zara looked around. "Hey, guys, we need to get a move on. Let's try and follow the glacier down—" She broke off as a low rumbling filled the air. As the noise grew louder, a familiar voice echoed across the glacier.

"You will never escape me! Never!"

The rumbling became a roar. Aisha stared in disbelief as the top of the mountain seemed to slide closer. Blinking, she realised a gigantic wall of snow was falling from the top, straight towards them.

"Avalanche!" she shrieked.

CHAPTER NINE

There was no time to race for cover from the lethal wall of snow thundering towards them, spewing rocks and boulders in all directions.

"What are we going to do?" shouted Phoebe.

"Feather!" cried Lily as a huge slab of rock crashed down a short distance away. "Can you lift the rock? We could shelter under it!"

Feather stamped the ground with her hoof and pink sparks flew up. The slab rose into the air and floated against the mountainside, forming a roof. Everyone dived underneath it.

Lily murmured encouragement. "You've got

this," she said, stroking Feather's neck. "You can do it!"

The air seemed to vibrate as the wall of snow descended. It crashed down around them and for a while the noise was so loud, it hurt their ears. Aisha reached out for Lily, placing a hand on her arm in support as the snow thundered past them, slamming into the slab then pouring away. Feather's magic kept the slab in place. At

last, the thundering stopped, and silence fell.

Feather floated the rock away from them and laid it down on the glacier. The girls stared around them. Snow was piled up against the base of the cliffs in great mounds and rocks were strewn across the glacier's snow-covered surface. Even the frozen sabre-toothed bear had a thick covering of snow over its icy surface.

"Phew! That was close. Thanks for saving us, Feather," said Zara.

"Thanks, Feather," everyone chorused.

"Let's get out of here!" said Aisha.

"Stop right there!" The count's voice snapped through the icy air as he strode out of the cave beside the frozen bear. He held up his portable weather machine. "You're going nowhere."

"Really?" said Phoebe, her eyebrows

arching. "Let me introduce you to my unicorn, Shimmer. The real Shimmer, whose mane is a different colour at the moment but whose magic is just as powerful as you said. Shimmer, why don't you show him what you can do?"

Before the count could react, Shimmer struck the ground with his hoof and fired a bolt of energy magic into the fresh snow beside the count. The snow exploded. Shooting into the air, it fell down over the count, burying him completely.

He fought to get free from the snow. As his head and hands burst out, his fingers moved on the controls of his weather machine.

Feather quickly banged her hoof and her magic plucked the weather machine from the count's grasp. It soared towards the girls, landing in front of them. Zara grabbed it and pointed it at the count. "Let's see how you like

being frozen!" she cried, as she pushed down on the blue button.

"How dare you!" screamed the count. "How—" His voice cut off as a jet of water hit him and he froze, his mouth still open in fury.

The count's half-finished sentence echoed around the glacier. For a moment, no one spoke.

"We did it," Zara said, breaking the silence. "We saved Unicorn Island from the count."

Aisha bit her lip. "We … um… We haven't killed him, have we?"

"No. When magic and science aren't combined, the effects can be reversed," said Zara. "Mr Longnose taught us that in our tornado lesson. I guess you weren't listening." She grinned. "As usual."

Aisha pulled a face at her.

Lily looked relieved. "So, the bear can be

defrosted too? I know it was attacking us, but it was only doing what bears do and it doesn't seem fair to leave it frozen."

Zara examined the device in her hands. "There's probably a way we can do it using this but I'm not sure what button to press."

"Wait," said Silver. "Aisha, have you still got that pink diamond you picked up earlier? You said it could melt anything."

Aisha drew the jewel from her pocket. "Yes, it's here. Let's try it out on the sabre-tooth polar bear. But not Count Thornberry. Ms Nettles can deal with him."

"Good idea," said Silver. "Feather, can you use your magic to touch the bear with the diamond?"

"Hang on!" said Phoebe. "You're all forgetting something. We're stranded here with no way home. The last thing we want is

an enraged bear chasing us!"

Suddenly they heard a high-pitched whistling sound above them and glanced up.

A man was falling out of the sky!

CHAPTER TEN

"Watch out!" yelled Zara. They jumped back as the man landed with a plop in a pile of soft snow.

It was Mr Longnose!

Sitting up, his fingers closed on something in his hand. "Girls, what are you doing here?" he said, shocked. He clambered to his feet, his eyes widening as he noticed the frozen count.

"I knew it!" gasped Zara. "Mr Longnose is in league with the count and he's come to rescue him!" Zara aimed the weather machine at him. "Well, stop right there, Mr Longnose. You're toast – well, ice!"

"Wait!" Mr Longnose held up his hands. "Please, put that thing down, Zara. I can assure you I am not here to help the count."

Zara held the weather machine steady. "A likely story!"

"No, please listen!" begged Mr Longnose.

Aisha stepped forward. "Zara, wait, we should hear Mr Longnose's side before we zap him." She glanced at Silver. "It's really important to listen properly when people have something to say."

Silver nuzzled her.

Zara nodded slowly. "All right. Go on then, Mr Longnose. Explain yourself."

"Thank you," said Mr Longnose. "I was marking the projects you did while you were in detention. Aisha wrote about Count Thornberry, mentioning that he had a secret lab in the ice caves of the Diamond Glacier."

"Aisha!" Zara exclaimed. "We agreed not to

write things about the count."

Aisha blushed as all eyes turned to her. "Did we? I … um … can't have been listening."

The others groaned.

"Well, it's lucky you did," said Mr Longnose. "I'd suspected that the count was behind the extreme weather disasters ever since I found a notebook he'd written. It was inside an abandoned cottage near where the tidal wave struck. I didn't have any proof that he was responsible, though, and I couldn't track him down. His family castle was shut up and I didn't know about the secret ice lab until I read Aisha's report. I told Ms Nettles my suspicions and she allowed me to ask the magic map to bring me to the Diamond Glacier. I was prepared to confront the count, but it looks like you've done my job already."

Zara slowly relaxed. "So, you're not in league with him."

"No," said Mr Longnose. "He may be a brilliant scientist, but he is arrogant, vain and cruel. I love this fascinating island and I promise you that I would never, ever do anything to hurt it. As well as being an inspector, I am part of an organisation of scientists who are committed to helping protect the island. We've had our suspicions about the count for some time. Now that you've found him out, he must answer for the damage he's caused. Shall we go back to school, and then I can get the proper authorities to deal with the count?"

"That sounds like a VERY good idea!" said Phoebe.

"But how do we get back?" said Zara.

Aisha's eyes sparkled. "Zara, weren't you listening?" she teased. "Mr Longnose said he came here using the magic map, which means that the thing he's holding in his hand..."

"Is the little model that will help us get back to

the school!" finished Silver.

"It always appears when people use the map," said Aisha. "Or had you forgotten?"

Zara grinned, taking the teasing good-naturedly. "OK. Maybe I prefer it when you don't listen, Aisha!"

Silver turned to nuzzle Aisha's black ponytail and gasped. He lifted up a streak of red, green and silver with his muzzle. "We've bonded, Aisha! Look!"

Aisha squealed with joy. Putting her arms round Silver, she hugged him tightly while her friends cheered and their unicorns stamped their hooves on the ice. Even Mr Longnose smiled.

When they had all finished congratulating Aisha and Silver, Mr Longnose held out the little model of the academy. Clearing his throat, he said, "I believe we need to hold hands."

The girls swiftly grabbed hold of each other.

"You can probably just hold Moonbeam's mane," Zara said to Mr Longnose.

He looked almost as relieved as the girls!

"Wait!" Aisha squeaked. "Before we go, Feather, can you use your moving magic to put this pink diamond on the bear?" She pulled the diamond out of her pocket.

"Of course." Feather sent the crystal flying from Aisha's hand and dropped it on the bear's head. Immediately the snow on the bear melted and the ice began to crack. The bear shook its head and started to roar.

"To Unicorn Academy!" cried Mr Longnose hastily.

Aisha's feet rose from the ground and a moment later she felt herself spinning through the air. In no time at all, they arrived back at the academy, landing beside the enormous map in the hall.

Ms Nettles was waiting beside it with Ms Tulip and Ms Rosemary. "You're back!" she exclaimed. "And girls! What are you doing? I didn't realise you were in the Wastelands!"

"We were kidnapped by Count Thornberry!" said Phoebe.

"Right," said Ms Nettles crisply. "You had better come to my study and tell me exactly what has been going on!"

Between them, the girls and Mr Longnose explained everything. Ms Tulip barely waited for them to finish before she jumped to her feet. "My hero," she said, gazing at Mr Longnose.

Mr Longnose gave a modest cough. "The girls are the real heroes. They kept their wits about them when the count snatched them from the school grounds. They managed to escape from his clutches and they also stopped him from doing any more damage. I merely brought them home."

"What will happen to his weather machines?" asked Zara.

"Once Lysander is locked away, I shall return to his laboratory and personally see that everything is destroyed," said Mr Longnose. "No one is getting their hands on any of his equipment or notes. It would be far too dangerous."

"Well," said Ms Nettles. "I'm most impressed,

girls. Your bravery and dedication have saved the island. You have also learned a very valuable lesson." Her glasses rattled as she looked at each of the girls. "Never judge a person by first appearances. Mr Longnose, thank you for the work you have done and if, at any time, you fancy a change of profession I would be happy to offer you a job as a science teacher. I have had excellent reports about the science lesson you taught the other day from both the staff and students."

Mr Longnose flushed scarlet. "Well ... er ... I have to say I did find teaching that lesson surprisingly enjoyable, Ms Nettles. Maybe I will consider your offer."

Behind his back, Phoebe grimaced but Aisha chuckled. Mr Longnose wasn't that bad and anyway, in a month's time they would have left the academy and be heading for lots of new adventures!

Aisha and Silver

The day of graduation dawned bright and sunny with a crisp frost. Aisha was happy with the music and they'd practised lots but still her tummy fizzed with nerves. The unicorns were brushed, their hooves painted with glitter and their manes plaited with ribbons.

The first parents arrived as lunch was finishing and the dorms came out one by one to do their displays. Topaz dorm were before Amethyst.

"What if no one likes my music?" Aisha whispered to Silver as they watched the boys doing an acrobatic display on their unicorns' backs.

He nuzzled her. "Why wouldn't they? It's brilliant."

Looking into his dark eyes, Aisha realised that as long as Silver thought that, nothing else mattered.

As the first bars of her music floated into the arena, Aisha's worries melted away. The parents and teachers clapped in time to the beat. Feather

used moving magic to hide various objects which Moonbeam located using seer magic to help her predict where they were. Then Feather moved a pile of snow banked up outside the arena, building a giant snowman. While the parents watched, Silver turned invisible and he and Aisha rode to the centre to stand by the snowman's side. Feather stood back with a bow and Shimmer exploded the snowman with energy magic. As the flakes of snow floated to the ground, Silver and Aisha appeared as if by magic, the snowflakes catching on Silver's mane and in Aisha's hair, to the audience's applause.

After the displays were over, everyone congratulated Aisha on her music. The graduation ceremony followed. Aisha saw her parents clapping proudly in the audience as she went to get her scroll and her heart swelled. Afterwards, the students and parents mingled, ate and danced

in the hall, decorated by the students with stars, rainbows and twinkling lights.

"We did it," Zara said when, finally, the girls and their unicorns went outside to watch the fireworks. "We're guardians now."

"I can hardly believe it," said Lily.

"I'm going to miss everyone," said Phoebe, her eyes filling with tears.

"We'll still see each other," said Aisha.

"Soon," said Zara. "First sleepover is at my house!"

They hugged as the first fireworks exploded in the sky.

Silver rested his head against Aisha's shoulder as the sky came alive with glittering colours. "I'm glad we found your magic and graduated with everyone else," Aisha whispered. "But I'm even happier that Ms Nettles chose you to be my unicorn."

"Me too. We're going to have so many more adventures together. I just know it!"

Aisha turned and kissed his forehead just as a huge red firework heart exploded in the air. Silver stamped his hoof and suddenly he and Aisha vanished from sight. Facing each other in the middle of the crowd, they shared a special secret moment together as they watched the heart fall from the sky in a stream of glittering red stars.

PRINCESS of PETS

Animal adventures, friendship and a royal family! From the author of The Rescue Princesses.

Another MAGICAL series from Nosy Crow!

SNOW SiSTERS

THE SILVER SECRET

THE CRYSTAL ROSE

THE FROZEN RAINBOW

THE ENCHANTED WATERFALL